SYLVIA GODWIN

It All Went Bananas

Contents

I saw mom read the letter, and the blood drained from her face. Her eyes widened and her hand shook a little. I didn't bother asking her what the letter says. I already know. I read it first after all. I watched mom's face closely, wondering if she realized or would even acknowledge that this was her fault, maybe not totally hers but majorly it is. I watched her walk on shaky legs and sink into the couch, then picked up the phone. I just watched, which is all I had been doing since this whole nightmare summer began. She picked up the receiver and put it to her ear. We're one of the very few people that still own a telephone. She sat there still looking numb, eyes unfocused. Her thought seemed a thousand miles away, but then her gaze focused a little and she clutched the receiver a little tighter before speaking. "Primrose, stop talking, I need you to come to the house right now, something's happened" her voice broke a little when she added, "they're gone. We have to fix this." She listened for a little while more before she said, "alright" and put the phone down. It is funny in a twisted kind of way that that's who she called. Of course, that phone call wouldn't have been necessary in the first place if she had just done almost what she just did a few times. All they had to do was talk and actually listen to each other, but that was far beneath both of them. Now it seems they're determined to work together to fix it, too little too late if you ask me, but hey, it's never too late right?

I wonder how they're going to fix it though. After all, the wedding was supposed to be tomorrow. We have made all preparations, down right to the toppings on the cakes. I would know, I only had to run so many errands.

I still remember the day this thing all started. How could I forget? I had been nursing my own problems before this entire shitstorm went down, and everyone went bananas. It's hard to believe it was only a few weeks ago. With all what had happened, it feels like it should have been months. I looked around the sitting room and then dropped into one of the couches. It was the same one I was sitting on that very day, the day this nightmare began.

Chapter 1

Fenella Hannes is the most beautiful girl I've ever seen, which is kinda weird considering I never really noticed it. Not until this year, and she's been my best friend since we were 5. With a heart-shaped face, and ever twinkling green eyes, long black shiny hair and her full smiling mouth and that body that seemed to appear from nowhere when she came back from that Christmas break she went on with her grandma to Portland.

"Dude, you really should just tell her already and stop making googly eyes at her, its nauseating to watch." My sister Honey said as she dropped into the seat beside me, mug in hand and I almost jump out of my skin before my eyes snapped to where Fen was bent over with my baby sister, playing doll or whatever they call it with her.

"Will you stop that?" I snapped at Honey, trying to talk from the side of my mouth to avoid attracting any more attention, but she just scoffed and took a sip of whatever she had in the mug. She opened her mouth like she was going to press the issue more, and I narrowed my eyes at the cup and in a few seconds, steam started coming out of it.

Her "ouch" put a smirk on my face just as Janus and Jensen, aka the twins, shouted, "no fair, mom said you can't use your powers on us." My smirk widened, but I didn't answer. We all knew they were only complaining because they don't have much powers yet considering it builds up the older you get, and we get to full power at 18, which is when we hold the grounding ceremony for the Gryffin men that enables us share our power with our future chosen spouse if they so wish. Since I'm 16 and they are only 11, there's really nothing they can do. Even Honey at 14 can't do much. They can get me in other ways though. They always have. Those two are evil. I can see in their eyes that they are already planning something. I hope their plan misfires and hits Cedar. That's one movie I'd pay for a front row ticket to. Our enigmatic devil may care brother would probably roast them alive. Maybe not literally, but close. I know that sounds like a lot of siblings but that's not even all of us. There's ofcourse me, Jaeger, then in descending order there's Storm, Cedar, Honey, Jensen and Janus, otherwise known as the twins, then Twinkle who is the baby of the house. I fit somewhere between Cedar and Honey. If you're wondering what on earth kind of names we have, we've wondered too, but then we forgave our parents because, really, with names like Rogue aka mom and Krithik aka dad, I can't say that I blame them. They're definitely an improvement from their parents. So coupling our odd names and and the magic thing which the townsmen know somewhat about but not the full extent, is it then any surprise that we hold the status of weirdos in this Boring town? No, I'm not dissing the town. Yes, it really is named Boring, sister to Dull. No, I'm not making this shit up and what do you know, it is the most exciting place to live. At least that's what it says when entering town. Apparently my great great something grandfather and a few others escaped from Salem during the witch hunt and the then mayor granted them asylum here after some heroic deed, I can't tell you what. Dad loves telling that story we just never listen. Except maybe Storm. She's the smarty pants of the the family, which is probably why she's at some fancy university in Chicago riding full scholarship, good for her. So the people let my ancestors settle with them, but somehow were never really seen as part of them. People were always wary of them except for maybe a few people, and they are really few. Till date, we still get those wary looks in town though most of them knew when we were born and watched us grow up, we are still semi-outcasts. of course maybe we should have tried to blend in better and not just celebrated our differences and worn them like badges, but then, maybe they wouldn't have accepted us anyway.

Honey said, "I'm just saying, better tell her before it's too late. Have you seen the girl? Someone else will snatch her up while you're here dwindling your thumb." She left before I could respond. Good thing too, because I don't know what to tell her.

How do I tell my baby sister that I fear confessing my feelings to my best friend, because what if she doesn't return them? But then another quiet voice in my head said, "what if she does?" Praying not to lose my nerve, I called out, "Fen?" She looked up at me and I swallowed, working up the nerve to say something. Anything, even invite her to one of our usual hangouts, but words were failing me while she continued regarding me calmly. Waiting. A knock sounded at the door and I breathed out in thanks and immediately stood to answer it. I could have sworn disappointment flashed in her eyes before she looked down to continue playing with Twinkle, but I have to have imagined that.

I was already on my way to the door when it occurred to me to wonder who could be knocking. We don't exactly get a lot of visitors. Siblings and mom are home except Storm, who's at school, and Cedar, who is wherever Cedar goes. Dad went to oversee the cows and other animals, but then none of those people would knock. I deftly jumped over the array of toys scattered here and there and made it to the door unscathed. I pulled it open and was surprised to see Storm.I frowned. "Why on earth would you knock, too lazy to push the door open?"

She scoffed. "Your face is too lazy to push the door open," she said, and I made a face at her, but she just smirked and a deep chuckle pulled my eyes to the other side of her.

I immediately pulled up to my full height of 6'1 as soon as I saw who it was. Lucas Walton, at my doorstep. I don't know him personally, though I've heard he's half decent, but I've had the misfortune of running into his younger brother. Severally. That pompous son of a bitch, don't tell mom I said that, but he deserves it, trust me. He walks around like he owns the place, well maybe he's father either owns or has a share in almost half the businesses in town but, so what? That doesn't give him the license to treat people like dirt. I bit out, "what is he doing here?" Eyes still fixed on him.

"That's enough Jaeg," Storm said, shifting my gaze to hers. "Whatever you want to say, bottle it and don't insult my fiance."

It befuddled me for a moment before I bursted into laughter, choking out, "this is so great, mom's going to just love this," between chortle. The guy in question winced, but my sister just pushed me out of the way and went inside. I called out loud enough for the other siblings to hear me. "Someone get mom,

Storm's home and she's got a guest and big news."

I already know how mom is going to take this, the Walton's are everything mom hates. Wealthy, arrogant and overbearing. Like it's not enough that they have more money than they know what to do with. They have to put everyone else down to feel good. It doesn't help of course that Mrs. Walton has had the effrontery to bad mouth milk from our farm which, by the way is the best in all of Boring and Dull combined, but according to her we are low class and so can only produce subpar things. Mom gave her a piece of her mind that day. It was indeed a sight to behold, which is why I'm expecting world war III. This wedding is going to be awesome. Fen stood like she was about leaving and the sight of her reminded me I haven't even been able to confess my feelings to the girl of my dream, talk more of ask her out and my glee got knocked down a peg. Lucas Walton proposed to the daughter of his family's' mortal enemy and I can't even ask the girl I've known forever on a simple date. Of course he probably never lacked for dates, he probably never had to prepare what to say for 6 months, he definitely seems to have confidence in spades, being good looking and madly rich wouldn't hurt.

Chapter 2

om came out looking sleepy but less tired than before. The news is that she's sick. I'm honestly hoping it's not another baby. We already doubled up in the rooms, and I have no idea where another baby would stay. We're out of rooms. But from what I know, there's no way to ensure you have a specific number of kids. You stop at the number magic and universe decides. No form of preventive measure works, short of maybe removing your womb. I wonder how that would work.

Mom and Storm play catchup until she could no longer ignore the elephant in the room, aka Lucas Walton, so she sighed and finally asked, "alright Storm, who's your friend?"

Storm looked slightly nervous, but then she looked at him and he gave her a small smile and a nod and she seemed to stabilize. Her voice didn't even quiver when she said, "mom, this is Lucas, Lucas Walton."

Mom's eyes narrowed like she's trying to deduce the punchline. Her face turned even more frigid before she asked, "and what is he doing in my house?"

Storm calmly said, "I brought him to meet you guys, well, to officially meet everyone. Lucas and I are getting married."

Everywhere went deathly silent. Not even the twins dared make a peep. Fen, who had been ready to leave, sat back down to watch the drama unfold instead. Mom's explosion of "oh hell no!" sounded much worse in the silence and I winced and looked at Twinkle. Hopefully she doesn't repeat it. We're still working on distracting her from Dad's favorite curse word 'shit'.

Storm, however, didn't cower. She gave mom an apologetic shrug. "I wasn't asking your permission mom, we came to seek blessings from both parents out of respect and love for you guys, but not your permission. We're going through with this whether or not you like it," she said, calm as can be.

Mom couldn't understand exactly what was going on. Her mouth kept going open and closed like she couldn't quite find words. And trust me, that is no easy feat. Mom might be all of 5'4 but she's all sharp mouth and lean muscle and so fierce you'd forget her height in a heartbeat. She just doesn't do speechless, well, until now. Lucas stepped closer towards mom and said respectfully, "ma'am, I really love your daughter. I'm sorry if this feels like we're pulling your hand, but we refuse to let whatever is going on between you and my parents dictate our lives. It has nothing to do with us."

Mom regarded them both pensively, then asked, "and have you told your parents this?" In a calmer voice than any of us expected.

Lucas sighed. "My parents know. We're waiting for them to calm down to talk to them again."

Mom searched his face for a moment, eyes narrowed like she was calculating something, then said, " fine, why don't you come with your parents tomorrow after you talk to them, then we can all discuss plans for the wedding. When is it, by the way?"

The couple looked at each other with tentative hope. Storm looked more suspicious than hopeful. She looked like she was searching for the catch and honestly, so was I, but said, "in a month. We want to be done with it and take time for honeymoon before we both resume our respective jobs this fall."

Mom frowned. "One month is too small to plan a wedding."

Storm shook her head. "No mom, we don't really want anything big or elaborate. Just a small wedding. One month will be more than enough."

Mom smiled tightly at them and gritted out, "yeah that's great. Remember to come back tomorrow. Excuse me."

Fen and I looked at each other with an uh-uh expression. Everyone knows mom doesn't capitulate that easily, unless of course she really is pregnant and those hormones messed her up bad. But no one dared speak, even after she had calmly walked back to her room. Storm muttered something about going to see Luke's parents then also left with her fiance, which is still weird to say. My sister is getting married.

Fen finally left after her grandma called her and I asked if she could come over the next day so I could tell her something, but I should have known the universe will jinx me.

The next day, I got the early morning shift with the animals, so I was home around 2pm when the knock came. Honey got the door this time, but I still got a front-row seat as the drama unfolded. Mr. Walton swept in first in a black suit, a suit of all things. I don't know much about suits, but it looked custom made. I was just wrapping my head around this when

Mrs. Walton swept in, in an elaborate dress that looked like it'll probably be appropriate for a dinner with maybe the queen of England, not to go discuss wedding plans at your future in laws' place.

Mom was in the sitting room this time in a simple maxi dress I know is one of her best ones. The way her right eye was twitching as she watched the Walton's made me hold my breath in anticipation. Mom was pissed, and she was not taking this lying down, or well sitting. She stood and told the Waltons the most frigid welcome I've ever heard in the history of welcomes and waved them towards a couch. Mrs. Walton looked at it distastefully down her nose, like it might actually stain her expensive dress, while Mr. Walton gave a sniff. They both gingerly sat like they have something shoved up their asses. Storm and Lucas came in a moment later looking frustrated and exhausted, followed lastly by none other than Bernard Walton, looking so bored he put a whole new meaning to the word. Guess that talk wasn't as easy as the one here had been. Dad came in a moment later from having taken a shower. He welcomed the guests and offered Mr. Walton a handshake. The man looked at the hand for a few moments, nose turned up distastefully like he might have a lemon permanently stuck at the back of his tongue, before he reluctantly shook.

Dad pretended not to notice, but when I looked at mom, her eye was twitching in earnest now. Uh-uh o. Dad took the seat beside her and gave her hand a few discreet squeezes. She took a deep breath. Me, I tried to stay as quiet as possible in case they remember I was there and decide to send me away.

Mom, the dutiful host, stood with a perfunctory smile. "Can I get anyone anything to drink?" She said with a strained civility.

"Oh, don't worry your poor head over that. I doubt you can

afford anything we would like," Mrs Walton said dismissively. A groan came from the direction of Storm and Luke.

Mom had to pause for a few more seconds. I actually think she might have been counting down, then she spat, "excuse you?"

Mrs. Walton even looked to be preparing to repeat herself. No atom of self preservation, that one. Imagine insulting a full-blown witch in her house. I understand that the town people don't fully know what we are, but come on.

"I'll have some water if it isn't a lot of trouble, ma'm," Luke said, cutting off his mother. Mom took a few more deep breaths and went off, presumably to get the water.

Dad turned to Storm after mom had sat back down. "Well, young lady, I heard congratulations are in order." She got up and came to his outstretched arm with a smile. He tilted his head towards Luke. "And as for you young man, if I see a single tear in her eyes that isn't from joy, I'll turn you into a rodent and leave you out in the wild and we'll see how long you last." Luke visibly shivered and dad turned to hide his smirk. He couldn't really do that, but our guests don't need to know that. He bent and kissed Storm on the head. "You have my blessings, sweetie. As long as you're happy," he said with a smile, and Storm beamed in return.

But then Mrs. Walton struck again. "I'm sure that was such a hardship," she said.

Mom's eyes snapped to her again. "What's that supposed to mean?" She asked, clearly angry now.

If Mrs. Walton noticed, she didn't care because she continued, "everyone knows my son is such a catch and what an honor it is for your daughter to land someone in the class of my son. I'm honestly not still convinced she didn't use one of those your mumbo jumbo on him."

Mom stood abruptly, teeth clenched with storms of fury in her eyes, her petite body was almost vibrating with it, the very air around her was charged with electric currents, the single light that was on in the sorting room flickered a few times and the Waltons cast wary looks to it. "What did you just say to me?" Mom bit out through clenched teeth, but I guess Mr. and Mrs. Walton's self preservative radars must have come on because they remained silent, their eyes suddenly finding other places to focus on. Mom sat back down after a few deep breaths in the absolute silence of the sitting room.

Storm gave a nervous laugh and said, "so, about the wedding…"

"We'll be taking care of all preparations, of course. I'll be making some calls as soon as we get home and everything would be taken care of," Mrs. Walton said with her usual sniff.

Mom primly adjusted her dress over her legs and said, "absolutely not" in a voice that is only mildly calmer than before. Mrs. Walton looked at her, flabbergasted like she couldn't quite comprehend how someone would contradict her, but mom continued, "I will plan my first daughter's marriage," she said, in a voice that brooked no argument.

"But I have so many important guests coming, I'm sure some royalties will be there too, you know we are related to the royal family a few times removed, I have to organize everything myself to make sure you people simply don't muck it up with your poverty minded choices," Mrs. Walton blustered out.

The sound of the door opening distracted me from the unfolding drama and the sight of Fen at the door blotted out whatever it was mom responded with. I saw her take stock of the room and her face flushed slightly at all the people inside.

Movement to my left pulled my eyes there, and I saw I wasn't the only person who had taken notice. Bernard fucking Walton has suddenly perked up, his sight set on Fen, boredom replaced by a winsome smile on his face. He was seated closer to the door than I was, so before I could make a move, he was already at the door hand stretched towards Fen. The smile turned up a notch. She flushed as she shook his hand and I gritted my teeth with eyes narrowed at them. I had to work to control the fire that I could feel blazing just below the surface. This wedding preparation just lost its entertaining appeal. Like I didn't have enough problems fessing up about my feelings, I now have to have competition with Fen? I looked at them again with resentment. It might not even be a competition. See her already blushing for him, when I can barely get her to notice me as anything more than her friend. I turn into a blubbering idiot these days whenever she's around. How then do I compete with this? It wasn't enough that he had money. He also had to have looks, and I had to grudgingly admit he might have charm. Looking at them, I decided, I can't let him have her. No matter what it takes, he has to learn he can't always get everything he wants, money or not.

Chapter 3

“Y ou really should get your fire under control bro, the Waltons are here, remember? And I'm afraid you might accidentally on purpose set Bernard Walton on fire,” Honey said in a conversational voice like she might not totally mind seeing that. Of course, watching him flirt with my girl, I mean Fen, non-stop every time he's come over for the past week, I've been buying into the idea more and more. I've actually gone from thinking of it in passing to actively considering it now. My eyes narrowed, really considering it as Fen threw back her head and gave her tinkling laugh that always sets my heart racing, wanting to do anything to make her laugh again. My teeth clenched as Bernard's mouth curved in a self-satisfied smile. I wonder what he would look like if all his hair was to say, catch on fire and refused to die down till he goes bald. I wonder if he would still pull smooth moves then. I clenched my fist as I wondered If I couldn't actually get away with setting him on fire, who cares about him anyway?

Honey's snort snapped me out of it and I saw that slight smoke was already coming out of the wooden handle of the rake I was using to clear the grasses to create more space for the ceremony. The battle for the venue had been an intense one with mom advocating for the grounds around our house and Mrs. Walton for some fancy event place all the way in Portland, fortunately or unfortunately depending on whom you ask, mom had won the fight. I'm still not sure magic wasn't involved, but hey, you didn't hear that from me. My only problem is instead of using a spell to clear this thing up, she's making us do the work by hand and I've had to watch Bernard put the moves on my girl repeatedly.

"It's not yet too late you know, you can still tell her now before wonton fully sinks his hooks into her," Honey said while also looking at the flirting couple.

I didn't know what to say to that, so instead I said, "its Walton" distractedly.

She waved it away with a lazy swipe of her hand."Same difference. All I'm saying is, just ask, what have you got to lose?" She didn't wait for my response before leaving, which is just as well. I watched the couple for a little while longer before tearing my gaze away. I dropped the rake and stormed off toward the house, determined to be anywhere but near the happy couple. What have I got to lose? Only everything.

"You can't possibly expect me to allow her to wear this old and cheap thing to get married to my son and embarrass me in front of all my friends and relatives. Are you trying to turn me into even more of a laughingstock?" Mrs. Walton shrieked, gesturing agitatedly towards a white dress draped over a couch I'm assuming is the dress in question with the way mom's eye is twitching and Storm is sitting hunched over on the next couch looking like she might have aged 10 years, but this isn't exactly a new scene. The wedding preparation has been going on for 2 weeks and every day seems to bring a new drama. Today seems to be wedding-dress. Beats me why it's such a big deal though, I mean it's just cloth, but I have a feeling mom would stun my ass if I dared say that so I kept my opinion to myself and took a seat to keep watching the drama.

"That dress you're insulting has been in my family for generations, you mannerless swine," mom shrieked back at her.

Mrs. Walton made a not so elegant sound in her throat. "well, I can see your family having had this for generations. It looks quite aged and not in a good way. Are you sure it was ever white?"

Mom narrowed her eyes and snapped, "fine! You want white? I'll give you a white dress," then turned her narrowed eyes on the dress. My eyes widened in alarm when she pulled out her wand, mom uses a piece of stick we fondly call her wand to focus her normally chaotic magic, but she is too mad right now to be casting any sort of spell that is supposed to be subtle and not offensive. Magic works majorly with intent and I have a feeling that mom's thoughts are closer to murderous than calm and clear right now. I opened my mouth to stop her, but she was already muttering the words of whatever spell she wanted to cast, and I snapped my mouth shut. Interrupting her mid spell would be worse than letting her cast whatever this turned out to be. All four of us focused on the dress to see that the color is already brightening, it slowly turned a brighter shade of white, mom's mouth curved in a satisfied smirk but then it died immediately as we all noticed a problem, the dress kept brightening and getting whiter and whiter until we couldn't look at it anymore. A tingling at the edge of my senses propelled me towards the offending dress and I rushed to pick it up, doubling my speed towards the door. I dumped it outside just as it burst into flames. Mom looked horrified, Mrs. Walton satisfied, and Storm simply looked tired and like she couldn't care less. I surveyed the ash that is all that's left of the dress they were fighting over just a few minutes ago and shook my had at the adults that have been behaving like children before walking inside the house mom and Mrs. Walton are too much alike. Both are so stubborn, no side willing to give in even when they realize they were wrong. If only they would just put aside their pride and differences, they would probably make a pretty awesome team. Wait, where have I heard that speech before? Oh yeah, mom's given it to us several times. The twins, me and Cedar, Cedar and Storm, but it seems mom can't take her own advice, talk about hypocrisy. I wonder what she would do if I reminded her of that, but of course, wondering is all I do because I still like my head and all my internal organs intact and in the right arrangement.

I came back in to Mrs. Walton saying, "well that went horribly wrong. You can't even be whatever it is you're supposed to be, right? Why on earth should I leave the wedding preparations to you?"

My eyes widened. She didn't. Mom is very testy about her magic going wrong. Having not been born a Gryffin but got the name by marriage, she hasn't had magic all her life but doesn't like being reminded of it. It always makes her want to prove herself. Mom took a deep breath and aimed a tight smile at Mrs. Walton. "I'm afraid you might be right," she said, coming to stand before the offending woman. I kept my attention on mom, not trusting this acquiescing act one bit. "Why don't we have some tea and relax, then plan again? I think tensions are just running high on both sides," mom concluded.

Mrs. Walton turned up her nose, but nodded. "Very well, a little tea might help."

Mom didn't even seem to take offence at her tone, instead she smiled, and I officially became afraid. I hope she remembers she can't just poison her. Mom came back a few minutes later with our barely used tea kettle and cups, and set it down before Mrs. Walton, who poured herself a cupful and took a sip. Mom also took a cup, but I noticed she wasn't drinking. What did you do, mom? "So," mom said, facing Mrs. Walton, who had finished her first cup and was pouring another. "What was it you were saying about preparations?"

Mrs. Walton set down her teacup and presumably to respond. As soon as she opened her mouth to speak, she rip such a loud rumbling belch that despondent Storm sat up and stared at her would be mother-in-law in shock. Mrs. Walton slapped a hand to her mouth, eyes wide in horror. "Oh dear, didn't quite catch that," mom said, looking oh so innocent. Mrs. Walton opened her mouth again and an even louder belch rolled out, coupled with another obnoxiously loud sound that was definitely not from her mouth. We all stared at her seat, in the sound's direction, and she turned a color I'm not sure I've ever seen on a person. Mrs. Walton abruptly stood and with a weird hand gesture, probably now knowing better than to try speaking, rushed towards the door, more blaring farts chasing after her. Storm and I simultaneously turned to face mom, and she shrugged. "What? I don't know what's wrong with her," she said, going once again for that innocent look. No one bought it.

Another week passed, and I still hadn't asked Fen out. Every time I think I've gathered enough courage, I see her laughing with Bernard what's his face, and I wonder, if she's that into him, or since her taste apparently swings that way, would she be any interested in me? We look nothing alike except maybe in height. He's all blonde haired, blue eyed, golden look, and I'm all dark looks. Bernard follows his mother here every chance he gets and considering Fen and I are neighbors and she's mostly always here, my house seems to be their meeting point. Like they're trying to rub it in my face. Bernard never has to do anything while I'm always stuck with work, so I don't even have the time to run interference. Of course, it doesn't help that mom and Mrs. Walton not being able to agree on anything means they destroy things at least once before grudgingly agreeing on one thing or finding an alternative, and somehow I'm always stuck with fixing them.

Dad keeps disappearing. Cedar goes off to wherever Cedar goes. Storm constantly looks stressed and on the verge of tears, so as usual, it falls to me. I can't help getting resentful sometimes. I have my own problems, people, but then no one really cares about that. Mom could probably fix all these things with a spell, but does she do that? No. Apparently fixing your mistake in the non easy way builds integrity. I wanted to point out how it wasn't even my mistake, but one look at her face and I relented. I'm pretty sure fixing without magic wouldn't include a recalcitrant son, so I had given her a tight smile and done as I was told.

I was sitting in the room I share with Cedar, pondering my problems, when an answer came to me, so obvious that I wondered why I hadn't thought of it. I heard Fen's voice in the sitting room, perfect. Now would be an ideal time to try this. Since Mrs. Walton isn't here yet, it's likely Bernard isn't either. I quickly put my plan in motion and looked in the mirror. I'm not very sure what to make of my reflection, but I don't have to like it, right? Fen just has to. I made my way to the sitting room trying to instill that easy confidence in my step but probably failing, I can almost bet I look awkward as hell, but I tried to reassure myself that, you'll never know till you try, who knows, maybe she'll finally notice me.

"OMG, why on earth do you look like you are playing in one of those stuck up people's castoffs?" Honey exclaimed as soon as I walked into the sitting room. She was sitting on the couch closest to the staircase and mine and Cedar's room, which is downstairs beside the stairs. I shushed her, taking a cursory look towards Fen, and saw that she was still showing Twinkle something on her phone. Thank God for small favors. I gently sat on the couch next to Honey and she turned to me, looking perturbed. "No, really, what happened to you?" She said, then looking at my hair, she asked with a frown, "and why on earth is your hair looking like...? Her eyes widened and she whisper yelled, "are you trying to make yourself look like Bernard Wonton?"

Heat suffused my face. We definitely had Fen and Twinkle's attention now. "Its Walton and can you pipe the hell down?" I gritted out through clenched teeth.

She looked at me defiantly but her tone was lower when she said, "I don't care what his name is, but really, why on earth would you try to look like him?" I didn't answer, but I couldn't help throwing a surreptitious glance to Fen and saw her giving me an odd look I couldn't decipher.

I saw Honey banging her head on the headrest of the couch severally in frustration and bit out "what" feeling defensive.

She gave me a long look before she sighed and shook her head, muttering, "boys are so stupid" under her breath.

"Hey, what's that supposed to mean?" I snapped.

"It means that you should probably change out of those pants before you rip something, probably the family jewels. I don't imagine pants that tight are comfortable nor good for you." I night have argued, but she was right, the pants definitely weren't comfortable, I don't know what I was thinking. It took me about three attempts to get on my feet, but as soon as I did, a sharp rending sound ripped through the otherwise quiet sitting room just as the door opened and the twins walked in. My eyes widened in horror and immediately flashed to Fen, but she was looking anywhere but at me and biting her lip like she was fighting laughter. Honey had no such problem. Her laughter was the first to ring out in the silent aftermath of the rip. The twins were still looking confused, standing at the door. I really have to go change out of this quickly before even more people come in. Only problem is I'd have to turn around and flash everyone in the room to get to my room, unless I want to make this even more awkward and try to walk backwards. I decided to brave it. Thank God for underwear. As soon as I turned around, more laughter joined Honey's, and I walked out of there as fast as my tight pants would let me. I hurried into the room, shutting the door to their guffaw. I even heard Fen's pearling bells. Guess she lost that fight then. As soon as I change out of these contraptions, I have a sister to kill. I don't know what I was thinking, trying to get Fen to notice me like this. She had noticed me alright, as a laughingstock. A smile pulled on my lips as I remembered the sound of her laughter. At least I had made her laugh. That had to count for something, right?

Chapter 4

I was on my way to the chicken pen to clear out their shits, pick up the eggs if there are any and change their water and feed when a large truck pulled up into our driveway, followed by Mrs. Walton's car. It looked pretty expensive, too expensive for Boring if you ask me, but then no one ever thinks to ask me anything. Three men came down from the truck and started offloading things I realized were flowers under the directives of Mrs. Walton, right on the grounds around our house. I covered my face with a groan. This woman never learns. She thought the fart attack was bad? Mom is definitely going to blow a gasket over this. I watched, both anticipating and dreading what the outcome of this would be. Mom definitely won't take this laying down. I kept right on watching and waiting to see what would happen next, like watching a bad accident. I couldn't seem to help myself. I saw one of the men walk to Mrs. Walton with a clipboard while the others finished up the offloading. "Why don't you sign here for us ma'm, the decorator would be by in a few days with his team to work on the decorations and flowers," he said, she gestured for him to turn the clipboard around then held out her hand expectantly for the pen with a mild frown on her face, he hurried to put it in her hand almost dropping it in the process which just deepened her frown but she signed without any comment before dropping back the pen like she might catch some incurable disease just by holding the pen.

She surveyed the delivery before turning back to the man. "He had better have the place in top-notch condition before the wedding or else your company will hear from me," she said with that upturned nose look I'm realizing she gives almost everyone. The poor man was still busy stammering out reassurances while she turned her back on him and began walking towards the house. I guess he is too low on the class pool for her to acknowledge him or offer a simple thank you.

Mrs. Walton was halfway to the house when I saw mom stomping out of it, or as much stumping as a 5'4 petite woman could do. What she lacked in sheer size, though, she made up for in the fire of fury in her eyes and a stormy frown on her face.

Mrs. Walton must either not notice this or was pretending not to, because she said, "oh good you're here, saves me the time to find you or one of those children you seem to have all over the place. I had the decoration company send over some decorations, starting with the flowers." I took one look at mom's pinched expression and clenched fist and hightailed it out of there to the barn. Those manure would not pack themselves out of the chicken pen. Warring in-laws can either learn to survive or end up destroying each other.

Even after all these years of doing this work, the smell still packs a punch when I open the pen. The cluck of the chicken is soothing or irritating depending on the day and today leans towards the latter. It doesn't help that I can see Fen and Bernard outside. They just happen to be outside close to the barn I happen to be working in? Definitely Bernard's idea. Rub it in my face that he doesn't just have money, he got the girl. Wish I could set his stupid ass on fire, would be so worth the repercussions of harming with my powers.

The clearing of the pen might have taken longer than it should have with me looking outside every other second. Bernard's face with that smirk that seems permanently pasted there while he whispered things to Fen I couldn't hear. Hearing her laugh for him was the last straw. He had been standing with his hand on the post dad had put there for any items we wanted hung while working. My anger got the best of me and I glared at the post, willing it to heat up. Not enough to burn, well, maybe a little blister, but he's a big guy. I'm sure he could tough it out. Hearing him scream while looking at his hand in bewilderment was so satisfying, but the icing on the cake, he stumbled back and stepped right into the pile of manure I had been packing out to take to the field. The horrified look on his face looking at his shit coated designer sneakers had pulled the laughter out of me. It was satisfying to see him make a fool of himself in front of Fen. Then I looked at her, expecting to see her amusement, instead she was looking at me like I had grossly disappointed her and just like that, the scene didn't look so funny anymore. Bernard might not have realized why the post burned his hand, but Fen clearly figured it out. She knows me pretty well, after all. "Fen?" I called out tentatively as Bernard stumped off, red with fury.

For the first time in 12 years, she looked at me like she barely knew me. "How could you stoop so low?" She shook her head at me and also stormed off. I guess it was a testament to how far gone I was that I was still grateful it wasn't after Bernard but towards the house. Clearly trying to be like Bernard, whom she clearly wanted, didn't work, and making him look bad in front of her just gained him her sympathy. Maybe I should just stop trying so hard. What on earth am I doing? I know Fen better than anyone. We've been best friends for years, before I suddenly started making everything weird. Maybe I just need to approach her as me, her best friend. I haven't really tried to tell her as myself. I used to be able to tell her everything. Maybe I should try that again. If our friendship can't survive one, 'I would like to be more than friends' talk, then maybe it wasn't meant to last, anyway. With this resolution, I cleared out the pens and changed their feeds and water troughs while whistling a soft happy tune with a bounce in my step.

I almost ignored the commotion on my way back to the house with the assumption that mom and Mrs. Walton were at it again, but then I heard a shrill scream and changed direction with a sigh, wondering what it was this time. My eyes widened, and I froze as I rounded to the front of the house. Nothing I came up with had even been close to the truth.

Chapter 5

My brain was trying to catch up to exactly what my eyes were seeing, and failing. Mom was standing in the driveway, arms crossed, looking stubborn and unbending while Storm spoke rapidly to her, but that wasn't the disconcerting part. The driveway that had been mowed grass, with a few flower pots from Mrs. Walton's delivery when I went to clear the pen, could now only be described as a flower jungle. There, smack dab in the middle of the small jungle, was Mrs. Walton, wrapped up in flowers like an unwanted Christmas present. She whimpered, then screamed again, and I cringed at the shrill tone. I tried inspecting her, which is when I realized something else that gave me an even longer pause. The flowers, they seemed to be… alive. I watched one offshoot snap at Mrs. Walton's face like it was toying with her, then I took another look at the whole jungle and realized exactly what it was. Mom never learns, does she? Plant is one of her specialty. She can do other stuff, but plants are her babies, hence her deep knowledge of them, enough to know the right ones to give someone a fart attack, maybe. But that could be explained away as an accident. Not this, though. We're apparently throwing caution to the wind now and revealing our powers, because there's no other way to explain flowers and plants suddenly gaining a mind of their own and trying to… Strangle Mrs. Walton?

I match closer to mom and Storm. Storm's urgent words become no more coherent with proximity, but I heard words like fix the mess and get in trouble. I fixed my eyes on mom instead. I studied her face for a few moments before it dawned on me. "You can't really fix it, can you? It's not that you don't want to, you just can't." I stated calmly, interrupting Storm's rant.

Mom's eyes snapped to me and narrowed, "what are you doing here young man? Go to your room," she snapped at me.

I jutted out my chin. "What are you going to do about her? You know this is going to be a problem. I don't even know how many rules you just broke. What would you do if she suddenly starts talking?" I replied, still looking at her but trying not to look defiant. I have an opinion, not a death wish.

Mom took a step towards me, eyes narrowed, hands on her waist, and said with a growl. "You go to your room right this instant, Jaeger. I will handle the problem."

I snorted. "That'll be a first. We both know you've made a lot of messes since this wedding nightmare started." I said with an annoyed twist to my mouth. She looked thrown, and I hurried away before she got her wind back.

I'm honestly done fixing her mistakes. She's the adult. Let her take care of it this time. I have a speech to plan. How exactly do you tell your best friend that you've been in love with her for months? Mrs. Walton's shrill scream chased after me as I pushed the door open and let it swing shut behind me.

Words have never been more elusive than when someone is searching for what to say, so I decided to just wing it and say whatever comes to mind at the time and hope that I don't word vomit.

With my mind made up and slight jitters, I went towards Fen's house the next day. It's a trek I've made at least a thousand times before. Her having lived just across the field from us almost all of our lives, but today the trek seemed even longer. Looking around at the wild flowers and grasses, I can't help but appreciate the beauty of nature. I might be more connected to fire than most, but we are first and foremost connected to nature. My hand ran over the flowers as I passed by, wondering if I should have maybe tried to call Fen before going. With only about four days left until the wedding, it's rare to find any free time. I came out behind Fen's grandma's house. The familiar cottage brought a small smile to my face. We have so many memories here. I rounded the house and came to an immediate stop, even with the hot summer sun, my temperature ran cold, before I broke out in sweat, i felt like i had been sucker punched in the chest, there on the porch of the cottage stood Fen, with Bernard's arms around her and their lips locked. My chest suddenly felt too tight. I guess Fen had decided after all, I must have made a sound I wasn't aware of because Fen finally pushed him away and her eyes locked on mine. Bernard stood there with his arms crossed. Fen's mouth opened like she was about to make an excuse of some sort. I wasn't sure I wanted to hear it, though. Honey had warned me, but I guess it really is too late now. I turned away and traced the path that brought me there back, back, with my feet dragging and my heart heavy, I went home to find something to do. I'll take any form of distractions now, even fixing one of mom's messes. I had been in love with my best friend but had been dragging my feet, but now it's too late. I lost my best friend, anyway.

****

The universe is cruel enough to have nothing for you when you want something tangible to do desperately. I sat in our room, playing with my fire, flicking it on and off on my fingers trying to concentrate enough that it doesn't get away from me and catch on something, trying not to obsess over what I just saw, trying not to let it destroy me. The door pushed open, but I didn't bother to turn to see who it was. "Fen's here to see you," Honey said, walking deeper into the room. I kept right on playing with my fire in silence. "Did you hear me, bro? Fen wants to talk to you," she insisted.

I finally shrugged. "I don't feel like talking to her," I said as nonchalantly as I could, but she probably heard something in my voice because she finally walked around to face me.

"Is everything ok?" she asked, her voice softening, but I couldn't answer. I couldn't even meet her gaze. I shrugged again and went right on playing with my fire, looking at it like it held the secret to the universe. I felt her gaze on me for a few more minutes before she finally left, shutting the door quietly behind her. I remained in the room for the rest of the day, the rest of the family somehow knowing to leave me alone. Honey's handwork I guess. She can be a little busy body but she's always had my back when it mattered. Cedar didn't talk to me at all when he came home, but that isn't anything out of the ordinary, though the wrapped up chicken nuggets he dropped on my bed was. I looked up at him in surprise, but he ignored me and walked to his side of the room in silence. He's always been a bit of an enigma, but for the first time, I understood his language.

Chapter 6

I woke up with the nagging feeling that something was wrong. It was a day to the wedding and I might have thought it was just the thought of my sister marrying a Walton, but I had met Luke a few more times and had reluctantly agreed that he was different from the rest of his family. I kicked off my blanket and went to the kitchen to get a glass of water. I gulped the first down, then took the second to the couch, sipping on it slowly. I frowned at the crunch of paper under my butt and adjusted to pull it out. I saw Storm's writing on the paper, addressing it to mom and my frown deepened. I thought about going to wake mom and giving it to her, but I looked around. No one seemed to be awake yet, besides it isn't quite daybreak so I'd hate to wake mom if it wasn't so important. Just to make sure, though, I opened the envelope. It wasn't even sealed. I scanned through the content of the letter, my eyes widening in shock. Storm had really done it this time. I worried about how mom and the in-laws would react while simultaneously feeling proud of Storm. I could even admit to feeling a smidge of pride for my brother-in-law to be, or maybe he was already my brother-in-law by now.

Mom's usually over the top about some things, but she had taken it too far with the wedding preparation. I remained seated in the living room, sipping my water till I ran out, then just waiting for mom to wake up so I could hand deliver the letter. I wanted to see her expression when she realized exactly what she had caused.

I saw mom read the letter, and the blood drained from her face. Her eyes widened and her hand shook a little. I didn't bother asking her what the letter says. I already know. I read it first after all. I watched mom's face closely, wondering if she realized or would even acknowledge that this was her fault, maybe not totally hers but majorly it is. I watched her walk on shaky legs and sink into the couch, then picked up the phone. I just watched, which is all I had been doing since this whole nightmare summer began. She picked up the receiver and put it to her ear. We're one of the very few people that still have a telephone. She sat there still looking numb, eyes unfocused her thought seemed a thousand miles away, but then her gaze focused a little and she clutched the receiver a little tighter before speaking "Primrose, stop talking, I need you to come to the house right now, something's happened." Her voice broke a little when she added, "they're gone. We have to fix this." She listened for a little while more before she said, "alright" and put the phone down.

It is funny in a twisted way that that's who she called. Of course, that phone call wouldn't have been necessary in the first place if she had just done almost what she just did a few times, all they had to do was talk and actually listen to each other, but that was far beneath both of them. Now it seems they're determined to work together to fix it, too little too late if you ask me, but hey, it's never too late, right?

I wonder how they're going to fix it though, after-all, the wedding was supposed to be tomorrow, all preparations have been made, down right to the toppings on the cakes, I would know, I only had to run so many errands.

I looked up at the tap on my shoulder. Honey asked, "what's wrong?" quietly while rubbing off sleep from her eyes.

I crossed my arms and relaxed into the couch.

I fixed my gaze back on mom before I said, "Storm and Luke decided they've had enough and eloped to have a quiet ceremony. The wedding was apparently turning into something they barely recognized, same with their parents, and Luke hated seeing Storm so stressed. Well, that was the gist of it, anyway."

I more heard than saw Honey drop into the couch beside me. "Huh, I didn't think they had it in them," she said, leaning back on the couch.

I turned to her with a frown, "what do you mean?"

She shrugged. "I guess I can see the sense in waiting this long though. Can you see mom's face? She never expected anything like this, but then, I guess there are only so many times Storm could beg her to rein it in and cry secretly before they did something drastic. Me, I can't wait to see how they get out of this one." She said with an amused twist to her mouth, then narrowing her eyes at mom for a few seconds she turned to me. "You think she'll use to magic?"

I shrugged. "I don't see much good that'll do her, though. There's only so much magic can do, little things maybe. This is for sure beyond anything I can think of that they might do. They'd have to rely on good ole common sense and charisma." I also studied mom and added, "besides, look at her. I think she's finally back to her senses, and she feels terrible. I doubt she'll try to magic the problem away this time. She then wouldn't be able to cite it as an example for her favorite lessons, after all." Honey chuckled lightly, and we shared a look. I guess there's a reason we work so well together.

I eventually left mom to her brooding to carryout my morning chores. Mrs. Walton strode past me with a determined look on her face as I stepped outside. I guess she probably learned some kind of lesson too, with her and mom putting their heads together, I know they'll cook up something good. I just couldn't be bothered about what. I guess we'll see.

The sound of more people than could possibly live in my house and the ding of things hitting surfaces dragged me out of a disturbing dream where I was the officiating minister in a wedding between Fen and Bernard, good thing they woke me before it was time to kiss the bride, I don't think I could stand to see that a second time even if it was only a dream.

I stumbled out of my room bleary eyed and grabbed the first person I saw, which turned out to be one of the twins. I'm not awake enough to tell which. "What's going on?" I asked with a yawn.

He looked at me like I was crazy. "Its Storm and that guy's wedding," he said slowly, and I grimaced.

"I know that, but Storm and Luke aren't here, or did they come back while I was asleep?" I asked with a raised brow.

He shrugged, already looking bored with the conversation. "I don't know, mom said something about a reception." He pulled his hand from mine and continued his race to wherever to do God knows what.

I looked down and realized I was only in a boxer and sweatshirt and rushed back to the room to change, freshen up, then go find out exactly what's going on.

I ran tight smack into Fen in my haste to go out and find mom after changing. We both paused, looking at each other for a few seconds before I tried to covertly check to ensure her new boy toy wasn't close. I might be working on accepting that I had lost her, but I'm not sure I was at that point where I could take it being thrown in my face.

I opened and closed my mouth a few times before I got out, "hey, fancy seeing your here, how's the boyfriend?"

She regarded me in that calm, wise way of hers.

"First, fancy seeing me here? At your house? Really? And second, I don't have a boyfriend." My heart wanted to leap at that, but I forced it to stand down. I raised my brow, still looking at her, and she rolled her eyes. "Bernard and I aren't dating," she said, exasperation obvious in her tone.

I frowned. "What, you can kiss him but not date him?" I asked, voice dripping with derision. I saw that day again, the day I lost her. I don't know how many times I've relived it already in a two-day period.

She stepped closer to me, face turned up and eyes holding mine. "I never kissed Benard, he kissed me, i was so shocked I froze. By the time I pushed him off me, it was too late. You were looking at me like that. Like I could ever betray you like that. I know how much you don't like him. Why do you think I've been hanging out with him all this time?"

I swallowed dryly. I could hear what she was saying, but I was still afraid to hope. I looked away from her piercing gaze, looking towards the grounds where the decorating team was putting finishing touches to everything and shrugged. "I wouldn't blame you, you know. I could even get the appeal, maybe, if I really put my mind to it."

She griped my hand and my eyes snapped to hers to find them narrowed. "Don't tell me you just insulted me by insinuating what I thought you did just now," she gritted out. I wisely kept mute and she abruptly let go of me, paced a few feet away and came back."The only reason I hung out with him was because I just wanted you to react, say something, do something, anything, but you didn't." She said, voice laced with frustration. "Didn't you care?" she added softly.

My eyes widened, and I closed the space between us. I slowly brought my hand up, giving her plenty of time to stop me, but she didn't, so I tucked her hair behind her ear. "It was tearing me apart just watching you guys together. I cared way more than I should, too much, but didn't know how to tell you I was beginning to care in ways beyond friendship. I didn't think you even noticed me in that way and I was afraid if i confessed and the feeling was one-sided, things would get awkward between us. Then you started hanging out with him, and even though I hated his guts, I could actually understand it. I didn't like it but i tried to understand. I mean he could give you so many things i couldn't."

She wrinkled her nose. "You mean like an arrogant smirk and a presumptuous attitude? Yeah, he has a lot of things you don't." she said, with a perfectly straight face and I chuckled despite myself.

I looked at her in wonder, then ran my hand down her face and her eyes drifted shut before opening again. "I thought I lost you," I said softly.

She shook her head. "You couldn't lose me even if you tried," she said.

I cupped her face, and she leaned into my hand. "If only I had the guts to confess my feelings earlier," I whispered.

"And if only I had been more open about my feelings and what I wanted earlier, too," she whispered right back, and we both gave a wistful smile.

I don't know who moved first, but then my lips were closing over hers. I circled her waist with one arm and pulled her even closer, while the other threaded through her hair and turned her face up to deepen the kiss. I couldn't have described the feelings coursing through me right then if I tried, but Fen, in my arms, felt like sheer perfection.

A loud wolf whistle had us breaking apart, with the slight burn in my face I knew I was a flush, and I looked at her and saw that she was too but we grinned at each other and I took her hand and threaded our fingers, glad that I finally could without feeling weird. I gave her hand a gentle tug, "come on, let's go find my mom, I want to find out what going on." She immediately followed but said, "oh I already saw her. She said we're having some kind of reception. I guess all the people coming for a wedding are getting a reception instead with the news that the couple married earlier and are already on honeymoon."

I came to an abrupt stop in shock, pulling her with me, then bursted into an almost maniacal laughter. I chortled for almost a full minute before I could control it. I shook my head and cleaned the tears from my eyes. "Of course they did. I should have known that the both of them together would have surely twisted it so they don't look bad." I shook my head and continued walking, gently pulling Fen with me. She looked at me askance and I chuckled again. "Those two, I really don't know if I should hail them or be afraid."

She looked towards a section of the yard and i followed her gaze and saw mom and Mrs. Walton with their heads together and she gave a mock shudder. "I vote afraid. With those two finally working together, I think we should be very much afraid," she said.

I grinned and pulled her closer, unable to help myself. "You know, I think you might be right," I said with a smile.

She rolled her eyes. "I thought we already established it, Jae."

I frowned. "Established what?"

She smirked. "That I'm always right," she said triumphantly.

I laughed and pulled her into a hug. "Ok, I'll give you this one," I said in an almost convincing condescending tone and she stuck her tongue out at me before running off and I grinned and gave chase.

Epilogue

"Come on babe, just a little farther," I said, trying to tone down the broad grin on my face, so as not to look like a complete loony.

Fen stood resolute with her hands on her waist, refusing to budge. "That doesn't look like the way to our spot by the creek," she said.

"Well, that's because it's not."

She narrowed her eyes. "Why then did you say that where we were going?" She asked, eyes still narrowed.

I smiled. "I wanted to spend some time with you and didn't want my family knowing where to find me. Well, my dad does, but not the others."

She softened a little. "This had better not be some kind of prank Jaeger Gryffin."

I grinned, trying to look innocent. "I would never."

She scoffed. "Tell that to someone who doesn't know you, because that heated water balloon that exploded in my face just yesterday begs to differ."

I winced a little. "That wasn't for you, though. Come on Fen, I really want to show you this. Summer's almost over and I want to spend some time with you, just us, before we officially have to start senior year.

She smiled and finally took my outstretched hand, and we continued our walk. The place really isn't far now. I know she'll like it.

We finally stepped into the small clearing, and I watched Fen as her eyes lit up. The clearing is covered in wild, colorful flowers, making the place more beautiful than anything I could have ever decorated. Also, some of the flowers bring out these sweet smelling fragrance that makes you just want to suck on them. Hopefully, we don't encounter bees during our stay. "How on earth did you find this place?" She asked in awe, still looking around. "Its so beautiful."

I grinned but didn't answer because I know she didn't really need my answer. I spread the blanket and began setting up the picnic basket I hid here earlier. She finally rounded to me and saw all the plates I arranged on the blanket and her eyes widened even more. "Do you fancy some lunch with the view?" I asked with a small smile.

She made her way over to me in slow easy steps, her short shift dress plastered to her body by breeze, and my breath caught. I almost habitually beat back the thought that the view provoked, but then I remembered, she was mine now. My eyes snapped back to her face and realized that her eyes had darkened. She had seen me checking her out. Good.

She finally looked down at the plates up close and her eyes came back to find mine. "Just how many establishments did you hit up?"

I shrugged, avoiding her piercing gaze. "I was trying to

assemble as much of your favorites as I could. They're all in small quantities if that helps."

She looked at me with an emotion I couldn't quite identify shining in her eyes. "You already make me so happy, you crazy crazy boy," she whispered just before her mouth closed over mine. The novelty of being able to kiss her, touch her, hasn't quite dissipated, and still makes me quite giddy. I ran my hand up the curve of her neck and into her hair. I love her hair. I gripped it a little harder, just the way I've learned she likes it. She moaned into my mouth and I deepened the kiss. My other hand trailed across her body, touching her everywhere while our mouths continued to move together. It rested on the curve of her ass and gave it a little squeeze before trailing down to the point her short dress met bare skin. I glided my hand a little along her skin and she pushed into me, grinding against my already raging hard on. I pulled my mouth from hers to breathe through what felt like all the blood in my body going south to a single point. I wanted to make today all about her, but it was getting harder to remember that.

She tugged on my neck where she still had her arms, gently pulling me down on the blanket with her. Her dress rode up even more and I could see hints of the pink lace underneath. I looked into her face and saw her hooded eyes gazing back at me. She gave me a small smile, then her legs spread wider, with her gaze still locked on mine. There's an invitation, and you didn't have to tell me twice. I dropped little kisses on her thigh, slowly working upwards. I licked at the top of her inner thigh, then keeping our gazes locked, I gently bit down, hearing her breath catch when I soothed it with my tongue. I tried to ascertain for the last time that she was okay with this. She nodded. I had only done this once before, but I had been researching. I slowly peeled down her lacy panties, licking suddenly dry lips as I took in the sight of her. I dropped a few more kisses on her inner thigh before I went straight in for the jackpot. I grabbed both legs and pulled her closer, then I closed my mouth over her clit, grazing it gently with my teeth and sucked.

Her back bowed off the blanket as she moaned. I released one of her legs and slid a finger into her. She was so wet it slid right in. I pulled out and introduced a second finger while flicking my tongue over her clit. She gripped my hair, her moan increasing in frequency, and I increased the pump of my fingers. I pumped into her furiously for a few moments, then gently bit down on her clit and her legs clenched on her head as she screamed her release. I gave her a few more kisses, then slowly withdrew my fingers, resting my head on her stomach as we both tried to catch our breath.

"We should probably eat all this food before they go to waste," she said after a while.

I smiled. "You'd never let good cheese dishes waste." I've never seen anyone as obsessed with cheese as Fen. Any dish with cheese immediately becomes a favorite.

"You know you're probably right," she said. "These have to have cost an arm and a leg," she added, running her hand through my hair.

I dropped a kiss on her tummy before sitting up. "Totally worth that look on your face." There's no way I'm telling her I had to do extra work to afford it.

She dropped a quick kiss on my lips, before opening the plates with an almost childlike glee. I smiled. Yep, totally worth it to put that look on her face.

Romance with a guaranteed happily ever after.

☐Please don't forget to leave a review. Even a simple, "loved it" would go a long way.

It All Started With a Peach

If you enjoy romance with a dash of the paranormal, then this is for you.

Storm Gryffin left Boring (the most exciting place to live) to escape her family's drama. What she doesn't expect is to see the son of her family's arch nemesis in school.

Storm's powers demands she maintain control at all times or things go wrong. Being near him is a bad idea, and now he wants her help?

Fated Accident

Escaping her father's tyranny was the goal. Laying low in a small town in the middle of nowhere, was the plan. Literally walking into some douche and making a fool of herself wasn't part of the plan. What's even more off plan is how he makes her feel.

Now she has to decide whether to stay or to run, because surely, her past will catch up with her and she wouldn't want to put him in danger, though it seems Caine has some secrets of his own.

She finds new information that makes her question everything she knew and realized that the little world she's built for herself might be in more jeopardy than she thought. Will she succeed in hiding forever, or would she be dragged back to confront her past.

Is It Too Late?

I know running is the Coward's way out. But I had to get out, I had lived with my secret and pain for too long, overhearing that conversation was just the last straw. Something happened, years ago even, I thought I was over it, but apparently burying bad memories doesn't make them go away. A lot has happened since then, now my new friend's in trouble and I'm forced to face my demons. I've finally realized, Its time to stop running and go home, hoping its not too late to tell them the truth and reclaim all I threw away, especially Ryan.